This book belongs to:

This book is dedicated to all nature lovers.
-A.M.

Meet April
Text and Illustrations copyright ©2023 by April Martin
Calendar Kids Books, LLC | Kathleen, GA 31047

ISBN: 978-1-957161-15-0 (Paperback), 978-1-957161-16-7 (Hardcover)
Library of Congress Control Number: 2023919024

To find out more about the Calendar Kids® Collection, visit www.calendarkids.com and sign up for newsletters or follow us on social media @thecalendarkids.

The Calendar Kids
meet APRIL

April Martin

This is April.

THE
END!

April lov—

THE
END!

The end? Wait... what? This story is just getting started!

"April Fools! Haha! Got you!"

Yes. You. Did. Now, where was I? Oh. That's right...
April loves to play pranks on us for April Fools' Day.

One year, she got her friends donuts, but when they opened the box, it was actually broccoli!

"yuck!"

Another year, she got her friends together after school for some brownies.

"Oh man! You are too tricky, April," her friends March and May told her.

"Oldest trick in the book," April giggled.

April also *really* enjoys springtime! One of her favorite spring activities is helping her mom make the best spring snack... dirt!

"*Mmm*, yummy! The perfect snack for a rainy day!"

April really loves watching a spring shower.
The new spring flowers soak up the rain!

She also likes looking for baby animals in her neighborhood.

One spring morning, she spots...

baby cows,

baby squirrels,

and baby birds!

She even has a jar of baby frogs, called tadpoles! Soon she will have to let them go. She is so excited to see them hop!

April really loves animals that hop, just like her pet bunny, Lily.
They work together to learn new tricks!

"Hop over here."

"Hop over there."

"Hop, hop, hop everywhere!"

This year, April is trying to show her bunny how to help her with the big egg drop contest at school. They need to come up with a way to save their egg from breaking when it falls to the ground.

They think...

and think...

and think!

"Oh, puddles. We are stuck. We need some help," April says to Lily. "Let's see if our friends have any ideas!"

The next day at school, March, April, and May learn all about Earth Day. Ms. Seasons teaches the class all the ways they can help take care of the earth.

"Every day is Earth Day!"

Ms. Seasons reminds the class.

Reduce

☑ We can buy used items instead of new. This helps use less plastic.

☑ We can turn off the lights when we leave a room.

☑ We can bring our own reusable straws with us instead of throwing one away every time.

Recycle

If we reduce and reuse items, we won't need to recycle so much. Anything we don't reuse, we place in our recycling bin and send it off to be made into something new.

Reuse

☑ We can drink from a reusable water bottle instead of one-time-use bottles.

☑ We can reuse boxes to mail items or put them in our compost bin to help make new soil for our garden.

☑ We can save glass jars for our art supplies.

After all their lessons on helping the planet, March, April, and May get together to plan for the big egg drop contest.

March thinks his egg will stay safe no matter what, because he is always so lucky! April shares her idea to use her bunny to help save the egg, but tells her friends she's stuck on what to make.

May shares her idea to reuse her garden flowers to help soften the fall.

"Oh, May! You gave me a great idea! Let's all look for items we can reuse to make our project, just like Ms. Seasons taught us!" April squeals.

On the hunt for the items they need for their project, March finds a cardboard box. "This should be good enough," March thinks.

March lost his pet again! If found call his mom.

Missing

Life cycle

frog

egg

froglet

tadpole

Reminder:
Egg Drop Contest 4/23

May fills an empty box of tea with petals and leaves from her garden to cushion the egg.

April looks through their recycling bin and spots an old Easter basket, bubble wrap, and a plastic bag. "I have what I need," she says.

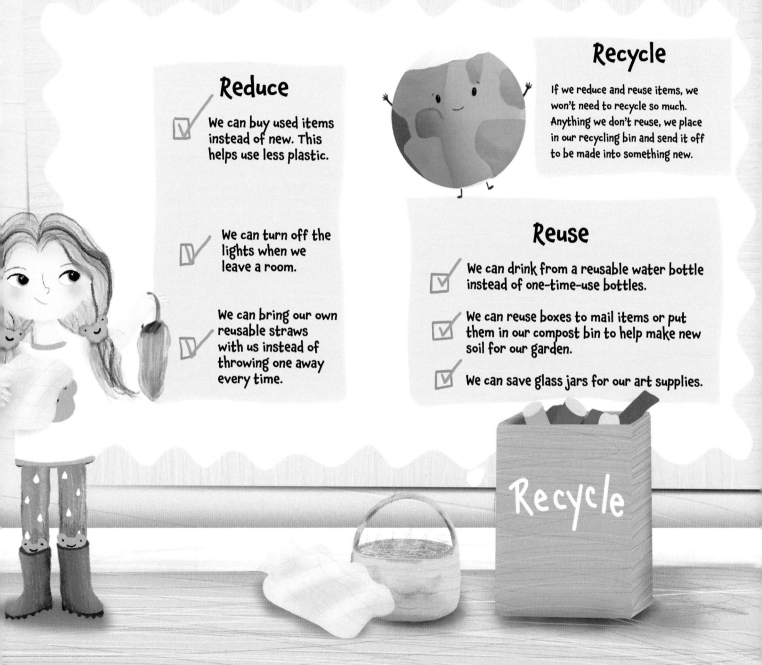

Reduce

☑ We can buy used items instead of new. This helps use less plastic.

☑ We can turn off the lights when we leave a room.

☑ We can bring our own reusable straws with us instead of throwing one away every time.

Recycle

If we reduce and reuse items, we won't need to recycle so much. Anything we don't reuse, we place in our recycling bin and send it off to be made into something new.

Reuse

☑ We can drink from a reusable water bottle instead of one-time-use bottles.

☑ We can reuse boxes to mail items or put them in our compost bin to help make new soil for our garden.

☑ We can save glass jars for our art supplies.

Recycle

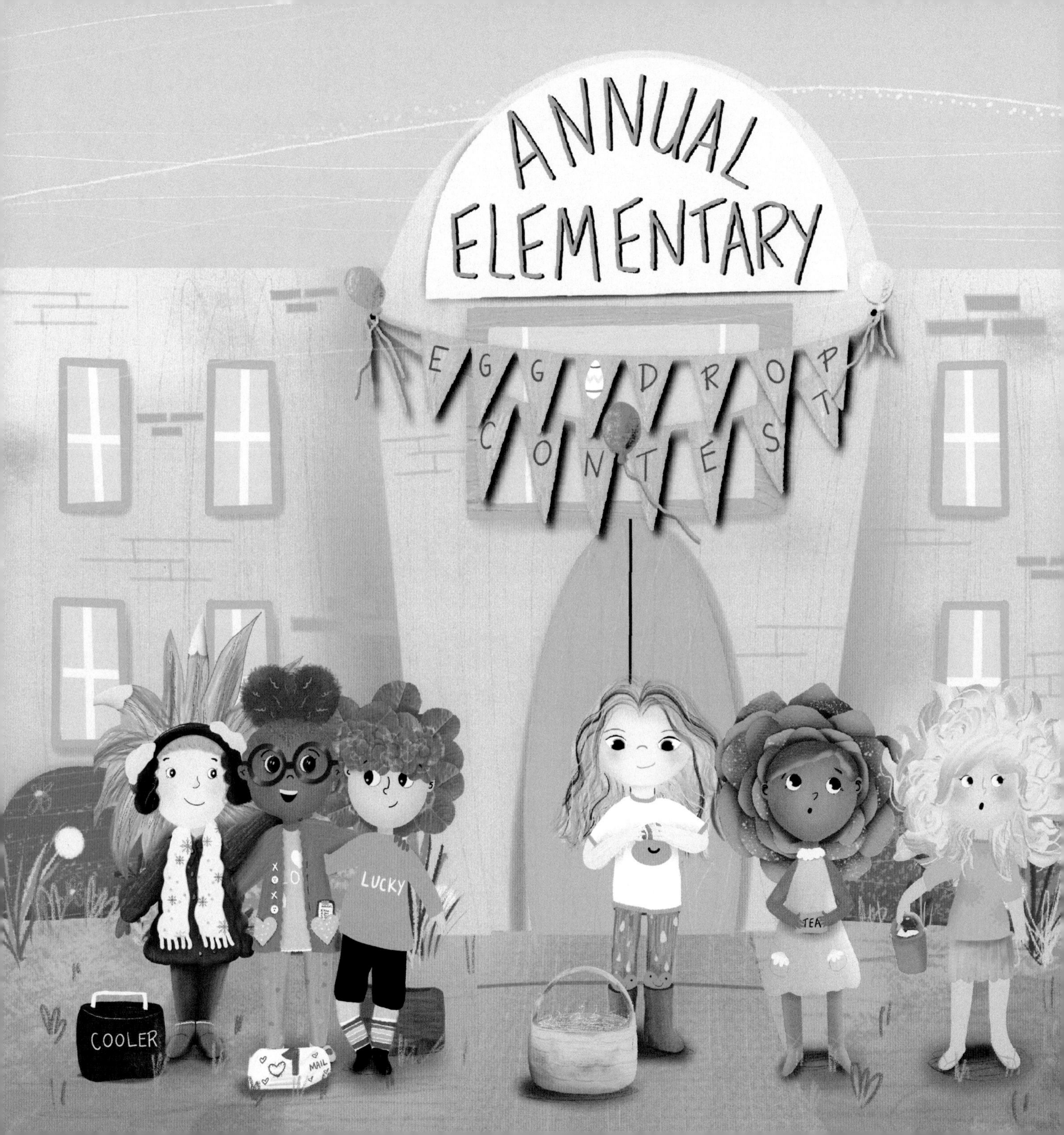
ANNUAL ELEMENTARY
EGG DROP CONTEST
LUCKY
COOLER
MAIL
TEA

The day of the egg drop arrives, and
the class lines up for the contest. They
are all ready to see who will win!

"uh oh!

Suddenly, a spring shower pops up out of nowhere!

"The rain is really coming down," March sighs.

"I love the rain!" April shouts. "It's my favorite! Come on, Lily, let's get ready. It's almost our turn!" April puts on her raincoat. She helps Lily with her coat and rain boots too.

"Hippity hop time!"

March drops his egg, but the cardboard box he used fell apart in the rain. "Not my lucky day," March says.

Then, May drops her egg. Her box fell apart, too, but she snuck in a secret backup plan. Her egg was wrapped up in the tea bags. "Whew, close one!" May says to March.

Next up was April. She was thrilled! She came up with a last-minute plan!
April tied the egg drop project to her umbrella and counted to three.
1... 2... 3!

HOP!

Lily hopped as high as she could and caught the egg just as planned.

They carefully opened the package, and their egg was safe! "We did it!" April cheers.

The rest of the class had their turns, and Ms. Seasons chose the winner of the contest.

"I award this year's egg drop winner to… April! She came up with a quick plan to save her project from the rain, and she even reused items like we learned about in class!"

March, April, and May walk home after their fun day at school. "It's about time to let my tadpoles go. They now have legs! This rainy day is a great day for them to find a new home. Come with me and watch!" April tells her friends.

April tips the jar over and lets go of the tadpoles she raised. One by one the tiny baby froglets hop away.

All but one.

"Oh, hello little friend! Do you want to play?" April asks.
"We love to hop! Come on, let's go!"

"The end!
For real this time."

My April Notebook

Special April birthdays or events in my family:

The best part about the month of April is...

April is the fourth month of the year.

The month after April is May.

April 1st is April Fools' Day. April 22nd is Earth Day!

April is a spring month and has 30 days.

Other April holidays that are sometimes celebrated are Easter, Passover, and Ramadan.

April is the Month of the Military Child. We recognize children of military families for their sacrifice and bravery.

If you are born in April, your birthstone is the diamond.

April is Autism Acceptance and Awareness Month.

Discussion Questions

1. April loves to play pranks. Have you ever been fooled on April Fools' Day?

2. What do you love about spring?

3. Have you ever seen a baby bird's nest in the spring?

4. Can you tell the five stages of a frog's life cycle?

5. Ms. Seasons taught the class about Earth Day. Name one way you can help the planet.

6. One way to help the planet is to reduce, which means to limit the amount of items we use. Name one item you can reduce the use of at home.

7. What type of clothing is April wearing? Name one item you use on a rainy day.

8. March's project fell apart from the rain. What is one way he could have prevented that from happening?

9. Do you have any good ideas for the egg drop contest? Name some items you would have used to win.

Visit www.calendarkids.com for more resources.

Dirt Pudding Recipe

You will need:

1 3.4 oz package of instant chocolate pudding mix
2 cups milk
1 container of frozen whipped topping
10 chocolate cookies, smashed or crumbled in a bag
30 gummy worms
1 mixing bowl
1 spoon
8 small, clear cups (so you can see your worms, of course!)

Directions:

1. Whisk pudding mix and milk in the bowl until blended.
2. Let sit for up to 5 minutes until the mixture thickens.
3. Gently stir in the whipped topping with a spoon.
4. Place cups on the counter to fill. Sprinkle 1 spoonful of cookie crumbles in the bottom of each cup.
5. Spoon pudding in until it is halfway up the cup.
6. Sprinkle another spoonful of cookie crumbles on top.
7. If you have more pudding, spoon on top or make another cup.
8. Place 3 to 4 gummy worms on top.
9. Add the rest of the cookie crumbles.
10. Chill until ready to serve. Refrigerate for up to four days.

"Happy birthday to me!"

meet APRIL

April loves looking for baby animals in the spring. Each year the pond in her yard has tadpoles and suddenly baby frogs are everywhere! Her favorite spring activities are starting her garden, watching the rain help the plants grow, and making dirt pudding for her kids.

Fun fact: April cares about the planet. She uses a compost bin and reusable items every day to reduce the amount of trash in the world.

Learn more about meeting the author and the rest of the Calendar Kids at www.calendarkids.com.

Made in the USA
Monee, IL
26 December 2024

75356360R00026